KATIE MORAG
and the TIRESOME TED

High Farm

The Holiday House

Mrs Bayview's

The Lady Artist

The Redburn Bridge

The Village

THE ISLE of STRUAY

Grannie's

The Mainland

The Jetty

ISLE of STRUAY
SHOP & POST OFFICE

OBAN
TIMES
GET
YOUR COPY
HERE

The Shop & Post Office

ALSO BY MAIRI HEDDERWICK IN RED FOX

Katie Morag and the New Pier
Katie Morag and the Two Grandmothers
Katie Morag and the Wedding
Oh, No, Peedie Peebles!
Katie Morag and the Big Boy Cousins
Katie Morag and the Grand Concert

A Red Fox Book

Published by Random House Children's Books
20 Vauxhall Bridge Road, London SW1V 2SA

A division of Random House UK Ltd
London Melbourne Sydney Auckland
Johannesburg and agencies throughout the world

3 5 7 9 10 8 6 4 2

First published in Great Britain
by The Bodley Head Children's Books 1986
Red Fox edition 1999

Printed in Hong Kong

RANDOM HOUSE UK Limited Reg. No. 954009

ISBN 0 09 911881-5

To All Bears - Mine Especially

KATIE MORAG
and the TIRESOME TED

Mairi Hedderwick

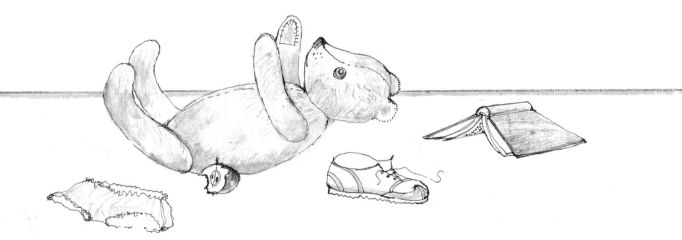

RED FOX

There was great excitement on the Isle of Struay. Mrs McColl at the Post Office had had a new baby, and everyone was delighted.

Everyone, that is, except Katie Morag. She had been in a bad mood ever since the new baby had arrived.

"No one talks to *me* any more," she grumbled to herself, "or brings *me* presents."

"Don't worry," everyone said knowingly. "Katie Morag will soon get over it."

But Katie Morag could not and would not get over it. She kept doing naughty things, like stamping her feet and nipping her little brother, Liam. One day she was so cross that she stomped all the way down to the jetty and kicked her friendly old one-eyed teddy bear into the sea.

"Tiresome Ted!" she shouted, as he disappeared into the choppy waves.

Mrs McColl was at her wit's end. "How can I cope with running the Post Office *and* with looking after the new baby *and* Liam, when Katie Morag is behaving like this?" she asked, throwing her arms up in despair.

Mr McColl said that he *was* trying to help.

ISLE SHOP

SEAMEN'S STRIKE ON

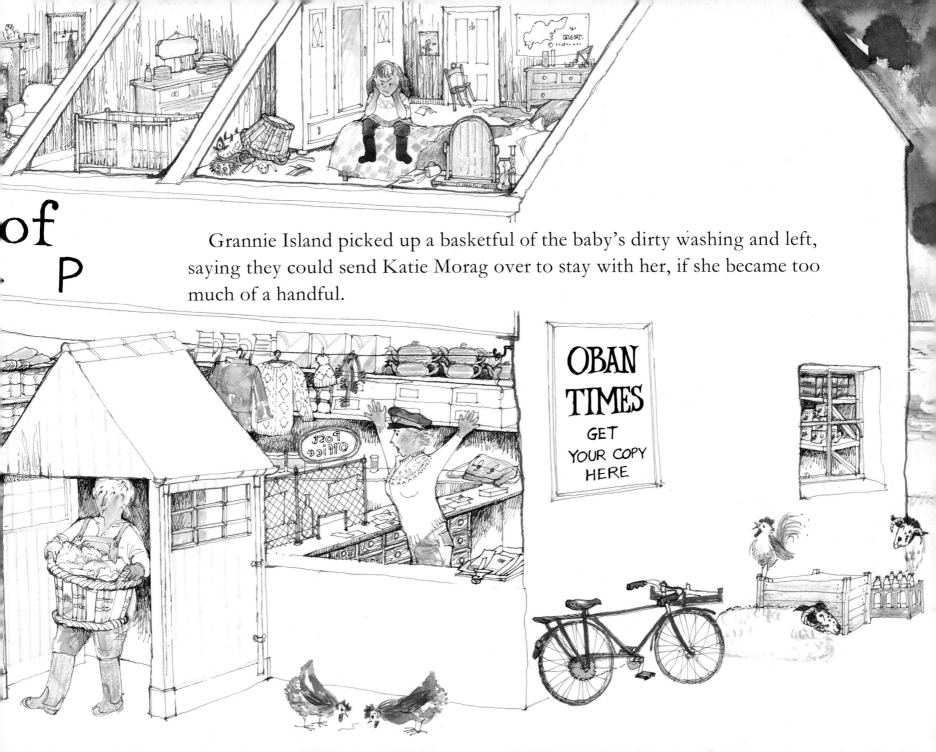

Grannie Island picked up a basketful of the baby's dirty washing and left, saying they could send Katie Morag over to stay with her, if she became too much of a handful.

POST OFFICE

OBAN TIMES

GET YOUR COPY HERE

That night the first of the winter storms battered at the window. Katie Morag could not sleep. She wondered what had become of her old teddy and she began to wish she hadn't thrown him away.

She crept over to Liam's bed and took his hot-water bottle . . . but it didn't make her feel much better.

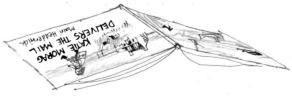

The next morning things seemed even worse. Katie Morag woke up to a wet bed. Liam thought it was very funny, but Mrs McColl was furious. It was the last straw.

"I think perhaps Katie Morag should go to Grannie Island's for a few days, after all," sighed Mr McColl.

Katie Morag trudged slowly over to Grannie Island's on the other side of the Bay.

"Having bad moods is very tiring," she thought to herself, and so engrossed was she with her own crossness that she didn't notice a familiar object being flung up by the waves of the incoming tide.

The bad weather lasted for two whole days and nights. Grannie Island could not get on with the washing, and Katie Morag was forced to stay indoors. She wondered how everyone was back at home.

And all the while her old teddy bear lay abandoned on the beach in front of Grannie Island's house. He was a sorry sight.

At last, the rain stopped and the sun came out. Katie Morag felt much better and she decided to stop being in a bad mood. She went down to the high tide-line to collect driftwood for Grannie's stove.

Katie Morag found all sorts of other interesting things that had been washed up by the storm: a ball for Liam, a box for Mr McColl, a bottle for Mrs McColl and a beautiful, big conch shell.

"I'll give this to the new baby," thought Katie Morag, "and show her how to hear the sea."

It was only then that Katie Morag noticed the two furry arms sticking
up through the seaweed. She couldn't believe her eyes. Old Ted wasn't
lost, after all.

Katie Morag rushed back to Grannie's and dried her teddy out by the stove. She filled his tummy with some fluffy sheep's wool and then laboriously began sewing up the large tear in his tummy.

Buttons

But even with his new eye on, he still looked the worse for the wear. When
Grannie Island wasn't looking, Katie Morag took something out of the
washing-basket.

The journey back to the Post Office seemed to take ages. Katie Morag couldn't wait to get home to show everyone the things she had found down by the shore.

The other islanders were pleased to see Katie Morag looking like her old self again. "She's got over it," they all said, nodding their heads.

"Thank you for the lovely presents, Katie Morag," said Mrs McColl. "And thank you, Grannie Island, for doing all that washing."

"It's good to have our Katie Morag back, and to see Old Ted again," said Mr McColl, smiling.

"I'll never, ever throw him away again, or call him Tiresome Ted," said Katie Morag, and she meant it.

And nobody said a thing about the missing Babygro from Mrs McColl's washing-basket, which was perhaps just as well.